STARS LIKE FIELDS OF CLOVER

CJ ERICK

Published by Water Dragon Publishing
waterdragonpublishing.com

ISBN 978-1-969655-59-3 (Trade Paperback)

FIRST EDITION

10 9 8 7 6 5 4 3 2 1

STARS LIKE FIELDS OF CLOVER

T HE RUSTED MOUND OF METAL lay half-buried in the waist-high grass like a dead elephant. After a careful examination from a safe distance, Beverly Nautilus concluded it was not pachyderm, but of a bee. She was delighted and intrigued.

Who left it there? Why? Was it part of an off-beat theme park? A hippie sun god, out there in the remote Hill Country? There were no climbing bars for kids, no covered shelter within for a fire and hookah party, no entrance of any kind she could see. And why here? She knew of every registered bee farm in Texas and there wasn't any for at least a hundred miles. She had come across the sculpture only because she was walking the craggy rock hills of this ranch, owned by the family of one of her employees. A photography hike in a place she'd been to several times. How had she missed the sculpture on previous hikes?

Its surface wasn't rusted, actually, more like the glazed patina that sometimes develops on a good aluminum fry pan. It glowed copper in the late afternoon sun, about three hours until sunset this late in May. She'd meandered over the grassy prairie for hours, thinking about rattlesnakes (and by association, the last fellow she dated several weeks earlier). There was time to check this strange thing out, get some shots, try for some weird light effects—ones that were interesting even before she attacked them with Photoshop.

She flicked the Nikon on and a hum far bigger than that from the camera blossomed around her, deep and harmonic, with a resonance that would have rattled her teeth if it had been above the bare threshold of hearing.

Was this a real hive? A real giant hive?

She eased backward, feeling her way. Bees would be drawn to sound. And probably infrared. Africanized, maybe. There had been a killer bee swarm the summer before in the small town of Seminole about two-hundred miles northwest from where she skulked, a town out in the middle of the Permian Basin desert. Luckily, no people had died, although it seemed dogs may have suffered.

The thing hummed louder, and part of the surface pushed inward and to the side—a door—revealing only darkness within. Suddenly she felt like she'd backed into an alien invasion movie and the large bulb-like head of a green Martian invader was about to come bobbing out of the dark rectangle.

Nothing came, except a faint tone when the door stopped moving, apparently fully open.

Then a voice—melodious and in a foreign tongue—spoke from the open door.

She ran.

•   •   •

But curiosity is a powerful thing, and the following Saturday she returned, lying to herself that her intention was to capture the nature photos she'd not gotten the week before for her company's summer sales catalogue.

The bee sculpture was there. She circled about it at the safe distance of several dozen meters in her trendy waxed-canvas hiking shorts and shirt which crunched as she moved. The fragrances of the flowers all around were so intense and inviting she could almost see them in multi-colored wisps, as if she enjoyed kinesthesia, as she longed for in her romantic childhood dreams.

The door was closed. She circled closer as if investigating a suspicious dish of sweet-smelling water. When she was within thirty feet or so, the voice came again; this time not just in her ears but in her head, as by some absurd aural-cranial form of kinesthesia. The words were still foreign, but within it was imploring, something heart-felt and universal. The sculpture wanted something from her and was struggling to learn how to ask in the right way.

She stopped pretending that her hiding was at all effective and strode up to the thing.

"What do you want?" Her voice sounded small and mouselike in the open air, as if mice had voices really.

Nothing happened for several breaths. How did time pass for the thing as it contemplated its response? Was it a fast and blurry stream of images, as she imagined it was for most insects? Or did it drip along in languid puddles like cotton-filled tar, as hers often did? Or was it merely a mundane series of electronic pulses?

The voice came again, still foreign, yet somehow less so, still touching her brain, but delicately.

Speak more, it said, or maybe that's the thing she wished it to say. A divorced woman wanting conversation, not such a rare thing, was it?

"I'm only here to take pictures. Is it ... agreeable for me to take pictures of you?"

She called it "you"? Because it spoke, she assigned it an identity?

Speak more, it repeated. Wow, this thing might be the perfect date, at last someone who wanted her to talk and wasn't completely enamored with its own blather.

"Okay. I'm a forty-five-year-old mother of three challenging, but ultimately rewarding children, two boys and a girl, none living at home now. I'm founder and CEO of an online antique furniture retailer, so that's where the photography comes in. I'm an athletic but somewhat geeky six-feet one-inch in stylish flats and do please interrupt me because I'm remembering how much I hate talking about myself—"

You may stop, the thing said, in unaccented English, or really in an accent so like her formerly Midwestern one that she couldn't hear it, probably.

"Hmm, I'm not sure I want to stop. You seem a captive audience, and maybe that's your purpose. I'm fantasizing this whole thing. A giant freaking bee sculpture in a field where only wildflowers, fire ants, and literal serpents should reside--"

I need your help, the bee said.

Words caught in her throat like chipotle pork taco

and she gagged. Had she just started to spill her guts to a big lump of metal?

Nothing else happened. She thought about running. She didn't.

"How? Why?" she said at last.

They come and I have no ... pilot.

Wait, whoa. Oh no, this wasn't some last space pilot ... movie pilot. She could handle her BMW 5 Series SUV all right, but she wasn't her mother the copter jock ... so forget the cyber-punk machine fighter scenario.

They come, it said again, with the sense of finality and doom that froze her ten-inch Gore-Tex-lined Sherpa hikers to the hard dirt.

"Who is 'they?'"

An image filled her head then, video without sound. She watched things approach through a dark sky with the bright speckles of stars behind. With no reference points, they might have been the size of cucumbers or buses, kids' toys or some rich adult's deep sea bathyscape. The resemblance to her new mentally-beaming mechano-friend was obvious. Large heads with two round fragmented eyes, eyes which despite having no lids or brows or the ability to narrow in outrageous indignation, conveyed anger. Their body segments were thicker than the bee's, and their wings longer, swept back tightly to their bodies. They were chunky and robust, like killer whales in space.

Hornets. Like those recent invaders from Japan. Murder hornets. Dozens of them. Gliding through the openness of space with a field of stars behind them, like the printed pattern one would find on one of her brother's creepy childhood bed comforters.

They come, the thing said again.

"How do we know they're coming here? And why isn't this in the news? Doesn't our government know?"

And how would this contraption answer that one? When agencies didn't even communicate with each other, how would this thing, this whatever it was with a talking computer chip, find out anything? By hacking the US intelligence agencies? Everyone else seemed to be, so maybe that wasn't as difficult as it sounded. Even her son had broken into a defense department satellite tracking station, and ended up having a recruiter visit him during his junior year at UT. That seemed to be the federal government's standard recruiting model; hire all the hackers that busted into their systems. Give them a choice to go to jail or join them and work for low pay.

"Why me?" she asked.

The thing hadn't moved at all, besides sliding its door open that one time. Maybe it was a joke, some kind of hidden camera prank. But why out here? It sat perfectly still, yet with a greater intensity somehow.

You are the one who hears us, it said.

There was a note of sadness in that voice, probably created by some translation algorithm to duplicate human emotion to affect a sub-conscious level. Damn if it wasn't working even though she recognized the trick.

She'd always loved insects and bees in particular. Once she'd stepped on a bee while dancing barefoot through a field of clover. She'd cried as her father, the former air force mechanic and college entomology professor, pulled the stinger from her sole with tweezers. He assured her the pain would go away soon, but she told him she wasn't crying because it hurt, but because the poor bee had lost its stinger and was going to die.

"No," she said, backing away again. "Find someone else." She turned and walked away steadily, glancing back over her shoulder only once to see it still anchored firmly in the grass, cupped by a foot of hard dirt, like a piece of cosmetic jewelry, a rough metal stone in a bad jewelry setting.

She stopped for one picture, then hiked to her car and drove back to Austin. She would not let herself be lured there again. Let the military fight the murder hornets if they came.

•   •   •

That night, she dreamed about attending an entrepreneur's business workshop in the sweaty summer in Chicago. She was naked and she couldn't find the meeting room, but a beautiful giant bee landed and carried her off to a land of milk and …

She woke to the sounds of angry voices and car horns in the street in front of her downtown Austin townhouse. Morning light came in low and flat through a crack in the curtains. The table clock read 6:02 a.m. She'd chosen this townhouse because of the quietness of the area, broken only weekly by Sunday church bells. But it was Saturday and someone was rudely sowing the seeds of chaos during her most important beauty sleep, and that would not make for a pretty image when she went to the mirror.

Her third-story window offered an unimpeded view of two city policeman and a tow vehicle driver standing with hands on hips surveying something parked in the loading-only spot in front of the townhouses. Joining them were several gawking onlookers, who were "Keeping Austin Weird" by dressing in everything from a man in black leather with a warlock's cape to an elder gray-haired woman in a Victorian dress to a young couple in pink running suits.

Resting at the curb, taking up two complete loading-only spaces and a couple feet of street, looking like a tarnished Airstream camper, was the bee sculpture. Seen from above, the shadows on the bee's surface brought out the outlines of wings held tightly to the thing's body, and tufts of antennae and hairs sprouting from its head and gaps between its massive body segments.

One of the cops had his cap pulled back exposing the white upper band of his otherwise well-tanned forehead and was gesturing toward the thing like an Italian grandmother in a bad Mafia movie. The wrecker driver was talking in a loud frustrated voice, shaking his head, and gesturing like the Mafia grandma's younger sister.

Beverly slipped into a jacket and jeans and took the steps down to the first floor, pushed the apartment house's front door open, and stepped into the fragrant and wonderful morning air. The cops and wrecker driver cast a glance her way, but then ignored her. She was in a mood to make that unconscious level of disregard and dismissal a capital offense.

"What's the problem officer?"

The head cop glanced up at her again over his glasses. "Nothin' for you to worry 'bout, ma'am."

"Looks like you're about to tow my car, so I think that's my worry."

"You own this thang?"

"Let's just say I may be responsible for its current location."

The cop struggled to decipher that one. "It's parked illegal, ma'am."

"How so? It's street worthy. It's against the curb. What's the problem?"

"No unidentified blobs allowed in the street. And it's too big for its own lane."

They come.

The cops and wrecker dude didn't seem to have heard the voice that impressed itself in her head. She tried to ignore it.

We need your help.

"*We?*" she thought, hoping the bee could read her mind as well as speak to her.

There are others coming to fight. But they will not defend this world unless we are there to represent.

"You gonna move it or do we have to tow it, ma'am?"

The officer stared at her with crossed arms, like every TV cop she could remember who'd found someone doing something annoying and illegal, but generally harmless.

"*Never mind how you got here, but why me again exactly?*" she projected.

We hear each other, was the matter of fact reply.

"*What does that have to do with piloting ... whatever it is you are?*"

I do not require a pilot with skill. I require guidance and ... motivation to fight.

"*But I have no motivation to fight. I own a business. I have children. I capture the world in pictures. I sell furniture anonymously over the internet, for god's sake.*"

If you won't fight, you may not have a business, children, or a world to picture.

"All right, y'all. Load it up!" The cop waved the wrecker pilot forward. The small, wiry man looked over the bee sculpture with a combination of suspicion and terror.

An image came to her again. In this one, space murder hornets descended from a pink sky on a city with tall, green, wand-like buildings topped with fuzzy glass balls. The hornets spat red-hot beads of energy which exploded on contact, sending debris and fire arcing skyward. The city's inhabitants, human-like beings with an extra set of arms and bright orange skin, responded with blue beam weapons of their own with only marginal success, downing only one of the hornets as the city went up in purple flames around them.

"What the hell is that?" The second cop waved his arms and pointed upwards. "A UFO?"

Beverly was afraid to look. When she did, she saw something she never wanted to see then or ever again. But it was there, a huge shining thing gliding across the sky, with narrow, orange, swept-back wings, tapered black body sections, and faceted yellow eyes covering most of its bristled head.

This was outlandish. She wanted to giggle, albeit maniacally.

A spy, said the voice in her head. *Others will arrive soon.*

A streaming collage of images and thoughts ran through her then, these her own thoughts and not something the bee imposed, coming to her in a flash as if she was drowning. Her children; her friends; the name sign above the front door of her business offices; photos she'd taken of beautiful flowers and landscape; her brother and parents; more images of her children, this time younger and playing with Star Wars toys, her daughter Chelsea being the most aggressive of the three—now a businesswoman herself with a child on the way. A day spent in a field of clover when Chelsea at age four had suffered a bee sting just as Beverly had at her age, but the daughter stoic about it, uncrying. And finally, the images of flying wings of hornets striking down on the weird emerald city and its orange-skinned inhabitants, who were losing the fight, dying by the hundreds.

The hornet made a second pass, this time lower and slower, arrogantly, as if fearing nothing from the little people scurrying and squabbling in the relatively ugly streets of the gray and tan concrete city beneath.

"Wait!" she shouted at the wrecker driver, who was leaning out the window and backing his rig toward the bee. "I'll move it!"

"Too late, ma'am." said the head cop.

But before the wrecker could move in, the ground trembled and the giant bee pushed itself to its feet on six thick, black metal legs. Wings unfurled, transparent and wide with thin shiny strands, like restaurant canopies made of cellophane, pivoting so the morning sun struck them over their entire surface. As the shaking stilled, a quiet hum took its place, growing in volume until it was more than just a note in her mind's ears.

This was all the wrecker driver needed. The truck groaned as he dropped it into forward gear and it lurched back out into the street and sped away, with the cops yelling in its wake.

I am waiting, said the bee.

"Fine. Open up."

The cops had retreated to their squad car and were busying themselves with yelling into unseen radio sensors and gesticulating with ever increasing levels of urgency. As Beverly approached, the door slid aside revealing the dark inner world she had only glimpsed earlier, a cave pierced by a series of small, bright lights in red, blue and white, which felt bizarrely and inappropriately patriotic.

Defend her country and the world? She was doing well to defend her company from her ex-sister-in-law's hostile takeover bids. When she stuck her head in the door, soft white lights streamed along a walkway like the lights on an airport runway, guiding her forward.

What was she doing? She pulled back out of the bee. The cop saw her hesitancy and was already on a radio. "I don't give a crap what that jackass said," he yelled into his phone. "Send another wrecker muy pronto."

Something flashed above and three more strange craft glided across the sky, dark, stocky, ominous, silent like the quiet that comes before a tornado hits.

They are here. There was a mechanical sadness in the voice that couldn't be explained by her perception of an algorithm. *They will seek fields of vegetation and sunlight. They come in threes, then threes of threes, until they dominate. They will devour. They will destroy. They will leave only carnage and death when they depart.*

They came in multiples of three? One, then three, then nine, then twenty-seven, ad nauseum? The three turned west, for the rolling fields in the Hill Country, where fields of bluebonnets, Indian paintbrush, and Mexican hats were just reaching their peak.

How do I do this? she thought at the mind of the bee craft. *Follow the white lights.*

An image of a cramped alien cockpit came into her mind, with a single throne-like metal chair in the center, crowded by panels and gizmos all around.

She breathed deep to quiet her heart throbbing like a plucked bass fiddle in her chest. She could feel her blood pulse all the way to her ears, her fingers, her toes. A headache threatened, and the encroaching black circle of an aural migraine drew its dark border inward from the edges of her vision. She climbed into the doorway, staggered, focusing on the white lights, a distance too far it seemed, until she came to the tiny chamber of the control room, where there was indeed a chair, something like a heavy throne, which she could barely see in the dark and only by the dim reflected running lights.

The pilot chair was too long in the seat and too narrow in the shoulders, and the arm rests too high, but when she lowered her tail into it, it was a perfect fit for her tall, thin body and limbs, as if designed for her.

To her unspoken thoughts, the craft said, *You are a child of the Keepers.*

"What does that mean?" she said aloud.

The Keepers. You are One of those who built us.

More images flooded her pounding brain, this time another world of bright yellow sunlight, huge flowers in every imaginable color and she knew she was seeing in the infrared range and possibly ultraviolet. More human-type beings moved among apartment-building sized buildings, where swarms of dark insects spiraled and entered, and others swarmed outward, flying away over the fields.

While she sat stunned, watching in wonder, soft, pliable sleeves rose from the chair arms and cradled her forearms, wrists, hands. She jerked her arms away.

"What are you doing?"

There was a pause before the bee answered.

We are connecting to you so you may guide us.

An image came of one of the Keepers, a woman similar in stature to her, but with stunning yellow skin and dark bristles for hair and ears, seated in the cockpit chair, her body shrouded by sleeves and what looked like heavy vests and headdress.

We will not hold you. You may rise at any time, if you must.

"I'm feeling confined. Don't you have any windows?"

Another pause, and then black shutters peeled downward, opening two great curving windows facing the street. Outside, another wrecker had arrived, a big one with a long tilting bed and chains, and the head cop was directing it backward toward them.

We must go. More of the marauders will come to this world. Your fighters will rise to meet them and they will fall.

"Okay." She laid her arms back on the arm rests, and calmed herself as the sleeves enshrouded her. Others circled her legs and feet, and a soft cap lowered onto her head, rolling down over her ears. She fought off a panic attack. Then nothing else happened.

"Now what do I do?"

Tell me to rise.

"Do it. Rise."

She felt a slight push in her bottom and legs, but the scene in front of them fell away. The wrecker's brake lights came on, and the cop jerked and tripped backward. Sounds of horns and people shouting came to her from around, but also other sounds she hadn't heard before; the hiss of a jet overhead, the noise of a city bus several streets away, the whoosh of leaves in the wind, the deeper buzz of the city, church bells miles away.

She felt as if she were melting and melding into the machine. She could no longer feel her own skin or hear vision was suddenly wide, so wide, formed from a matrix of smaller images covering the two spherical windows that began beneath her and swept back over her head and to each side. It was like sitting in the front of the mini-submarine at Ocean World, looking through the spherical observation glass, but being able to see in all directions at once. She felt her wings buzz and her claws clench and unclench at the sight of the hornets, but she felt nothing in her own hands. She had become the bee.

The three hornets hovered above.

It is time to fight.

"How? How can we fight three of them alone?"

Call the Hive.

"Hive? Where? How do I do that?"

The hornets all turned together, then raced away toward the west.

Ask me.

"Yes, fine. Call the Hive. By all means. Don't let me slow you down. Where are those things going?"

She willed the bee to follow, and they burst upward and after. She felt a humming vibration move through her like music, like a serenade or a swan song, a heat-wrenching, yearning turned acoustic. The hornets lanced ahead like air torpedoes, but she was surprised that they were not pulling away. This craft that she had become a part of was able to keep up, and in fact gain. Their song fell away on the wind, expanding outward from their wings and from vibrating plates in their abdomen.

"What could they possibly want?"

They seek to destroy all things necessary and beautiful for bees.

"Such as?"

Flowers.

"Shit!" The first annual Hill Country Bluebonnet Festival. Packed with all things B. Barbeque. Brews. Barrels (of wine and liquor). And the event's first director, Beverly's daughter, Chelsea.

"Don't come on day one, Mother," the ever-independent Chelsea had said. "I don't need you there trying to protect me."

"Faster, bee," Beverly said.

The rolling fields were carpeted in blue and purple, bluebonnets as deep and wide and thick as she'd ever seen them after the frequent rains and ample sun that had graced West Texas. In the blueness were patches of red and orange and yellow, the other wild flowers and clovers that competed every spring for southern exposure. Ahead, the hornets spread out in their triangular formation and dove nearly straight down, like suicidal dive-bombers in old war movies, or space opera craft attacking a rebel stronghold. But what could the attackers do to fields of flowers?

The answer came even as her thought ended. The hornets leveled out over the field and sprayed out a fog or fine mist beneath them, like crop-dusters. Where it fell, the multicolored carpet shriveled, turned black, and withered. Some kind of acid or defoliant?

She willed herself to dive after them, not sure what she was going to do when they got there. As the former president of the national beekeeper's association, she'd followed the stories of the Asian murder hornets and their appearance in the Pacific Northwest with a sense of dread. But those insects attacked hives and solo bees in the fields. They didn't attack the plant life they also required. These mechanical hornets didn't have the same needs and motivations, apparently. They just seemed to have come to destroy things.

She urged her bee to flatten out and aimed to head off the marauders. "What do they gain by killing the flowers?"

She felt the craft's artificial mind shaking its head.

There is no knowing with these killers. They seek to kill all bees they find. Why we do not know.

"Are the hornets like us? Do they have pilots like me within?"

Again, the bee shook its head mentally.

No. They are one as they are, driven by instinct.

"But they are machines or robots? They aren't live animals?"

There is no difference.

She was about to ask about the Hive, when blobby shadows crossed the ground beneath her. A dozen orange and black bee-craft followed in a double-V formation, all descending with her. Bee ships. But they were not as large as she was, perhaps a third smaller.

"Where did they come from?"

They were hiding on your world. Waiting.

"For these hornet things?"

They always come. Our makers sent us out into the heavens to protect.

She was nearly on top of the hornets. They were aware of her and the others, darting side to side and buzzing loudly in angry reverberations of hatred. The why of their conflict had become irrelevant. They were within sight of the town of Hye, Texas, where the main festival was being held. Several hot air balloons marked the fairgrounds where the festival was in progress, colorful targets.

"What do we do to stop them?"

We can do nothing without your leave. Give us freedom to attack them.

"Attack. Now."

The bees buzzed louder in harmonic cycles. People working the fields below stared and pointed and ran. As the bee chasers closed on the hornets, they extended their legs and claws. The hornets rolled into inverted flying, clacked their wicked claws and sprayed the deadly mist.

"Look out!"

The bees peeled off like fighter jets, narrowly avoiding the killer mist. One flew too close and the nearest hornet grabbed it, clamped huge pincher jaws around the bee's neck. One bite severed the bee's head, which the hornet threw to the ground. Beverly and her bee screamed as one, a tragic wail echoed by the others. Would they cry as each bee was felled? More than machines – were they any less than people? Was there a difference?

The hornet had slowed for the kill, and this proved a fatal mistake. Six bees surrounded it, grabbed and latched on, covering it in a cocoon of clambering bee bodies. Their bellies lit up in orange light like intense sun lamps. The hornet roared and spasmed and lashed out, knocking one of the bees away, but it was too late. Steam erupted from its seams, it thrashed, and then it froze like a dried cicada shell. The bees released it, and it nose-dived into scorched wildflowers and crashed in a shower of dark hornet parts.

The bees gathered in groups of three and harried the remaining two hornets in fierce sky battles. Three bees were struck and wounded by the hornets' red energy bullets before the two hornets were destroyed, one by the bees' roasting heat, and the other by having its wings and legs ripped off, a fall of a thousand feet to earth, and a killing evisceration by scissor-like bee jaws.

Carloads of people bound for the festival and the Hill Country wineries, bourbon distillers, and arts and crafts galleries stopped along the roads to watch the battle. How would the government spin away all of these UFO reports?

Beverly allowed her bee-self to breathe, when its voice engaged again.

The spy is escaping. We must stop it, or it will bring others.

"Where? Follow it."

The bee launched them straight up. Beverly was jarred back into her own body, once again just a tall woman in a tight rigid chair. The ground fell away, as well as the distant town of Hye, then three hot air balloons that had taken flight unwisely during the battle, and then wisps of clouds, like she was rising in a commercial jet liner, only much faster and straight up. She eased back into the virtual reality of her bee-body and sensed other bees following her, rocketing upward like mini-space shuttles on nuclear steroids.

An image came into her head of a single hornet soaring high into darkness—space! It was already escaping Earth's atmosphere.

"Can we go there?"

Yes.

She wanted to ask if she would be able to breathe in the vacuum, but they were already leaving the Earth's "most excellent canopy" of air, as Shakespeare had called it. She was still breathing. Question answered.

In space, with no air resistance, they weren't as fast as the larger hornet. It was getting away, heading toward the moon. The bees fired blue-hot energy beads, all of which missed or faded before they reached the target.

We must kill it now. It will use the moon to accelerate.
"How? Your missiles aren't working."
This is the thing we need you for. Help us.
She closed one bee eye and took aim, as her Texas father had taught her to do. Blue beads arced away and found the target, but caused no damage she could see. Too far away and too fast.

"We don't have any other weapons?" she asked, "like photon torpedoes or killer death rays?"
We have used all things. If we could catch it, we could kill it like the others.
"Doesn't look like we can."
The bee said nothing. It waited. For her. For guidance.
You own your own company, Beverly. You've overcome crises. Think!
Somewhere in her middle-aged brain was a memory flag, as she called it, a little white signal that waved against the inside of her eyeballs, a trick she had taught herself during business school as a way to remember tasks and meetings. But what was it for?
"Let's all shoot at once. On the mark ... fire!"
Ten blue beads lanced off into space at the bright circle that was the retreating hornet. There was a bright flash off the metal of the hornet's butt, but then nothing else. No satisfying eruption of fire and debris. No death wail of a dying bug.
Death wail? That nearly triggered the memory she needed. Something her older brother did when they were kids. Torturing insects with a magnifying glass.
A lens. They needed to form a lens. Their transparent wings. Several of them around her larger wings.

How many circles fit around a center one? Six. Yes. But she was slightly bigger, so maybe seven?

"Here's what we need to do."

She focused a mental picture of her plan. Almost immediately, her bee persona danced and spun in loops and circles, then lifted its wings above their head and curled them into a fair approximation of a flat disk. Several other bees joined them, linking legs and adding their wings to the growing circle.

She found the sun and pivoted as she continued to glide through space, feeling the other wings pressing in, wavering, losing connection, frustration, then cohesion again. Brief flashes of conical light burst out from their wings, flashes that would have blinded her in red afterimages and contracted pupils. But the bees had no pupils and no blood vessels in their mechanical eyes, so temporary blindness didn't come.

"Focus. Hold tight."

After several flashes, each longer than the last, a cone of white fire grew and held in front of them. But it was visible only within the first few yards as it lit the gasses and dusts from the bee bodies. In the vacuum of space, the beam was invisible. They would have no way of aiming.

"Sweep it slowly in a circle. Draw tight circles around the hornet."

The spy was now just a dim light in the sky, like a jet liner slowly fading into the distance. The team swiveled the beam around and around, in tighter and tighter circles. But the hornet's glow continued to recede.

They needed a guide, a pointer. What did her mother, the former copter pilot always call those things? Bullets that left a trail of light behind so the gunner could see where he was shooting? Teasers? No. Tracers. Yes.

"Bee—fire your energy gun along the light beam."

The bee hesitated, then a single blue bolt reached out in the direction of the hornet, missing to the right.

"Keep firing, every few seconds."

Blue bolts leapt out from them, this time passing above the fading dull glow she hoped was the hornet.

She willed the beam to circle in tighter. The hornet must have sensed danger, for it jerked sidewise a few degrees. Beverly guided the line of tracers like a curving string of crystal beads unwinding away from them. She felt like a bat must feel, trying to catch a swirling moth in the dark. So hard to do with the erratic motions of the moth. But in the end, the bat usually struck.

There was a bright flash of white and red, and a tragic squeal in her head. And then, when the fire faded and died, nothing. No bright spot. No rapidly vanishing light. No hornet spy.

Whew.

•   •   •

She left the bee in the field where she found it. She called a rideshare car to pick her up on the road where she had parked her vehicle the day before. To the silent inquiry of the driver, a young woman about twenty, probably a college soph or junior, she explained about her photography hobby and then distracted her from further inquiries with relentless questioning about the woman's degree plan.

In her mailbox, she found a parking citation from Officer Lou-Bob Blaylock. She paid it.

She was surprised, but ultimately pleased, that no reporters ever came to her apartment. But maybe a little disappointed as well. What's it like to pilot a space craft bee, Ms. Honeycutt? How is that you can talk to it? Can you talk to real honey bees as well?

Her daughter reported the festival had been a "smashing success," and even featured a wonderful airshow by some local flying group that never identified itself, a little mystery and growing legend for the Hill Country tourist trade. They expected the next year's festival to be even better attended because of the curiosity and interest aroused by the surprise aerial program. The official release from the armed forces confirmed joint war games from Lackland and Dyess air bases, offering non-committal responses to the many photographs showing the bees and hornets locked in deadly battle. Photoshop, they said.

On a Sunday several weeks later, she was awakened by loud voices and car horns.

Sitting in the same no-parking zone as before, the bee craft lay like a shiny hood ornament for some expensive British automobile. Officer Lou-Bob Blaylock stood at the curb, arms crossed, tapping the toe of his boot, shaking his head.

We need your help, it said.

"What is it this time?"

Locusts, was all it offered.

She laughed. Did bees laugh? She should like to find out.

"I'll be right down," she said.

ABOUT THE AUTHOR

CJ Erick's stories have been published by Abyss and Apex, Brilliant Flash Fiction, Water Dragon Publishing, Camden Park Press, and others. His short fiction received a recent Pushcart nomination and inclusion in *The Best Small Fictions 2023* anthology. He writes in multiple genres, publishes novels in a space fantasy series, and dabbles in poetry. He lives in the Dallas area with his wife and their rescue superhero dog Gretchenl, calls his sourdough bread starter "Ursula" (K. Le Guin), and cooks crazy-good Cajun food for a Midwest Yankee.

YOU MIGHT ALSO ENJOY

DINER ROVERS OF THE MILKY WAY
by Tyler Tork

The aliens came in 1950, but not to conquer —in fact, they didn't even particularly want to talk.

HAMM AND MEGS
by Gary Battershell

When Megan decided to go on a camping trip with her two college roommates, she had no idea that she would find herself involved in an alien plot to conquer Earth.

LITTLE GREEN MEN
by Curtis Bass

In an orbiting craft, Cooper has a front row seat to the first manned mission to Mars. Their landing is perfect until one crew member claims they are being watched by indigenous creatures.

Available in digital and trade paperback editions from
Water Dragon Publishing
waterdragonpublishing.com